The Mysterious Maze

RUBY PRITCHARD

The Mysterious Maze
By Ruby Pritchard

First published in Australia by Zhu Zhu Press 2025

Copyright © Ruby Pritchard 2025
All Rights Reserved

A catalogue record for this
book is available from the
National Library of Australia

ISBN: 978-0-6453709-6-6 (pbk)

Artwork and photography by Grandy © 2025

Typesetting and design by Zhu Zhu Press
Published in collaboration with Zhu Zhu Press

For Mummy, Daddy, and Sadie.
Nanny and Grandy.
Luna and Repunzel.

THE BEGINNING

On a dark rainy day, the 27th of February 2001 to be precise, five children: Jack who was nine, Harlow who was eight turning nine in a few days, Margot who was ten, Adam, who was nine, turning ten soon, and Kyle who was nine, were attending Kyle's grandmother's funeral.

On that day there was a storm and lightning, and it gradually got worse and worse, so they eventually had to leave. Kyle decided that he wanted to stay for a little longer, so when everybody else left, he stayed and sat by the coffin, trying to hold back his tears. Kyle was miserable, so sad that he started to cry. He cried and cried for ages until he got an idea. He remembered that he and his friends used to make spells and practice magic when they were much younger, and that his spell book and potions were in his basement.

So, he rode his bike to his house to go find the potions and the spell book. 'Um toad breath', no. 'Um bird's beak', no. 'Um spell book and liquid potions', 'YES,' said Kyle, looking at the book.

Kyle rode his bike back to the cemetery with his spells and wizard ingredients. He started spreading ingredients around the coffin and was nearly ready to try out his spell. 'Don't worry, grandma you'll be awake in no time,' he said while quickly skimming through the spell book for the right spell. When he found the 'revival spell', he opened the coffin to find no sight of his grandmother. 'Where's grandma?' he said. Instead of reviving his grandma, he was sucked into the coffin.

SEVEN YEARS LATER

'We have looked everywhere and there is still no sign of Kyle,' said Margot.

'What about over there?' asked Adam, pointing at the abandoned theme park.

They walked over to the front of the theme park, and the gates opened by themselves. When they entered the park, there was complete silence until Jack spotted a maze.

'Look guys, a maze, over there,' he said, pointing at the maze.

'I don't think that was there last time,' said Margot in a nervous voice.

'I have a really bad feeling about this. I'm going home,' cried Harlow.

'Same, my mum wants me home by five cause some of my family are coming over for dinner. By the way, I didn't mean that I was scared when I said same,' exclaimed Jack.

'NO,' Adam growled.

'Hey, don't raise your voice at us, Adam, we have done nothing wrong to you, so don't be rude to us. We are going home, NOW,' said Margot.

'Okay, I am sorry for being an idiot, and there are no excuses for raising my voice, but we will get back before five and if Kyle's in there and we don't go in, then we might never find him.'

'But what if we get lost?' asked Margot.

'We won't go far, okay?' said Adam.

'Okay,' said everyone else.

TRAPPED

They walked on the spikey gravel towards the maze, one foot in front of the other. They were getting really nervous and started to shake and get goose bumps, but not Adam.

They took one step into the maze and suddenly a cold gust of wind rushed through their bodies, making not just their hair blow, but it created a suspenseful feeling between each and every one of them, even Adam.

'I regret this. I'm going home now, and nothing can stop me, not even you, Adam,' said Margot in an angry voice.

'Same,' said Jack and Harlow.

They turned to leave to find a grass wall the exact same as all the other walls in the maze, blocking their way. Everyone turned around and looked at Adam.

'This is all your fault, ADAM!' yelled Jack.

'As much as I hate to say it, it wasn't Adam's fault, we chose to come,' said Margot.

OH NO HARLOW

After the teens got trapped in the maze, they decided to go and explore and look for an exit.

'Surely there's an exit somewhere. I mean, there has to be,' said Margot.

'I really hope there is because Harlow is starting to freak out,' said Jack.

'Are you okay, Harlow?' asked Adam.

'NO, I am definitely not okay. It is really freaky here, it's getting dark and there is a creepy spider wolf in that dark corner over there watching us, listening to us and probably wanting to devour us right now!' Harlow said, pointing at the spider wolf.

Everybody looked at the monster and screamed.

Harlow panicked and ran through the walls in a straight line, making a trail until they could no longer see her. The spider wolf chased her, but the others couldn't keep up.

'No Harlow, we have to go back for her,' cried Margot.

'No, it's not safe. We have to keep going. She will catch up don't worry,' said the boys calmly.

Margot didn't want to leave, so the boys had to drag her back through the maze to keep her back on track.

THE SNAKE LADY

As they slowly walked on the tiles in the maze, desperate to find an exit, all Margot could think about was going back and finding Harlow, but the boys just wanted to get out and go home.

'COME ON LET'S GO GET HARLOW. THEN WE CAN GO,' said Margot.

'No, we are so close to the exit. Harlow will be fine and it's past five now, Jack,' said Adam.

'Oh no, ma's gonna kill me,' Jack cried.

'We literally just left the entrance, which means that we are nowhere near the exit and it's only four fifteen,' exclaimed Margot.

They continued searching through the maze for an exit until they spotted another dark corner. In the corner there was a pretty lady, she was wearing a beany and a pair of sunglasses.

'Hey lady, you okay? Are you lost too?' asked Jack.

'Hello, my lovely children. My name is Maddie. Come here. I need to get a better look at you.'

They all took three steps closer to the woman and then she took off her beany.

'RUN. Don't look at her. Maddie must be short for…'

STATUE FRIEND

'MEDUSA!' screamed Margot in fear. They ran for their lives, following Margot.

'Medusa is a gorgon. Gorgons are monsters with snake hair and when you look into their eyes, they turn you into stone. They look like human when they wear sunnies and a beany, and some makeup to hide their ugly grins on their ugly faces,' yelled Margot.

'HEY I HEARD THAT,' yelled Medusa.

'How do you even know all this stuff, Margot?' asked Adam.

'My dad used to tell me bedtime stories about creepy monsters all the ti...' Margot said.

'Oh no,' said Adam.

'Oh no,' said Jack.

'H h h Harlow, HARLOWWW, NOOOOOOOOooooooooo. It can't be true, can it?' cried Margot.

Medusa had turned Harlow into stone.

'I have an idea,' said Adam. 'I will smash her, and she can break free,'

'NO. Let's get her out of here,' said Margot

THE DEMON DOG

They took Harlow and kept on searching for the exit. They walked over to another dead end with a sleeping puppy dog in it. It was very fluffy and cute, and it was so tiny that it was only on one little tile in the middle. Margot took one step onto a tile, ten tiles directly in front of the dog. Five tiles dropped, making gaps in between the other five still standing, then all the other tiles dropped, except for the five in the middle. Margot was on the first tile, the dog was on the last one, and Adam and Jack were in the corner holding Harlow, who was still in the form of a statue.

Margo jumped onto the next tile, and a bunch of darts shot from the walls in the corner, almost hitting her, but luckily, she didn't get hit, same with the dog, but she almost fell into the bottomless pit but just made it. Then she jumped onto the next tile and…

KYLE IS BACK

Nothing happened. She jumped onto the next tile, which was the fourth one next to the sleeping dog. The dog started to wake up, and then when it was awake, it was very mad. It turned into a CHIMERA.

'A Chimera is a lion with a scorpion tail, wings and two horns on its head!' exclaimed Margot.

It chased Margot, making every tile behind it drop.

Margot ran, and the boys followed her into a dark corner.

'Margot, Adam, Jack, is that you?' said a little voice in the darkness.

'KYLE'S BACK' yelled everyone, with Adam and Jack looking at him and Margot tearing up.

The chimera heard everyone yell and

found them. While it was in the middle of roaring, the boys ran away. Margot stayed to get Harlow, but the monster stayed, too.

THE ONE-EYED KEY

Right when the chimera was about to catch Margot, Kyle ran in and cut off the chimera's scorpion tail.

The chimera's instantly tail grew seven more scorpion's tails, and the monster raged and roared in anger as it chased them.

They ran to a door, but behind it there was a sleeping cyclops, which is like a human but only has one eye and is very strong.

The chimera roared, waking the cyclops from his nap. The chimera ran towards the kids, but they moved out of the way, so it ran into the cyclops. The cyclops wacked the chimera on the head with a spiky club.

THE END
or is it?

The teens were shocked, after seeing how careless the cyclops was about killing something although that thing was coming to kill him, so they didn't really blame him. The cyclops looked at the teens and they saw a key within his eye. Then the cyclops bolted at them, so Kyle jumped up in the air with his sword and cut out his eye. After they got his eye, they dissected the key out and opened the door and were finally free to go home.

Two days after they escaped, they had a funeral for Harlow. When everyone had left, Jack and Adam stayed behind. Jack remembered the 'revival spell' off by heart and stood by the coffin, about to open it.

'Jack, what are you doing? Let's go okay,' said Adam.

Jack agreed, but when everyone had left, he went back to the coffin.

Margot had forgotten her gloves and came back to the cemetery. She saw Jack open the coffin to find that Harlow was missing, and instead of reviving her, he might be the one who needs reviving soon.

'OH NO! NOT AGAIN!' said Margot.